Car

Written by Jo Windsor
Illustrated by Kelvin Hawley

Cat lived in Cargo Shed
Number One.
Carlos worked in the cargo shed.
He put boxes on the plane.

At lunchtime, Carlos gave Cat some food.
“Come on, Cat,” said Carlos.
Carlos sat and watched Cat.

In the shed, there were
big boxes, small boxes
and fat boxes.
Cat loved to play
in the boxes.
She loved to sleep
in the boxes.

One day, Cat was sleeping
in a big box.
Carlos didn't see Cat and he
put the big box in the plane.

The plane took off.
It went . . .

over the mountains,
over the town,
and over the sea
to Cargo Shed
Number Two.

CARGO SHED Nº2

At lunchtime,
Carlos called to Cat.
Cat didn't come.
Carlos could not find her.
Cat was lost.

So Carlos sent a message.

In Cargo Shed Number Two,
Cat woke up.
She was scared.

A woman looked in the box.
"What's this?" she said.
"You must be Cat.
I will send you back."
She put Cat into a box and
she put the box in the plane.

CARGO SHED Nº1
CARGO SHED Nº2

The plane went . . .

over the sea,
over the town,
and over the mountains
to Cargo Shed
Number One.
Cat went back
to Carlos.

Cat still loves boxes.
Boxes to play in
and boxes to hide in.
But when Cat sleeps,
she sleeps on a chair.
And Carlos calls her "Cargo Cat".

A Route Map

Guide Notes

Title: Cargo Cat
Stage: Early (3) – Blue

Genre: Fiction
Approach: Guided Reading
Processes: Thinking Critically, Exploring Language, Processing Information
Written and Visual Focus: Route Map

THINKING CRITICALLY

(sample questions)

- What do you think this story could be about?
- Where do you think this story is taking place?
- Who do you think Carlos could be? What sort of job could he have?
- Where do you think this cat came from?
- Look at page 8. Why do you think Carlos looks upset?
- How do you think Carlos could get the cat back?
- Look at page 10. How do you think the cat feels?
- Why do you think Carlos gave the cat the name 'Cargo Cat'?

EXPLORING LANGUAGE

Terminology

Title, cover, illustrations, author, illustrator

Vocabulary

Interest words: cargo, message, scared, shed
High-frequency words (new): watched, one, still, sleep
Positional word: over
Compound word: lunchtime

Print Conventions

Capital letter for sentence beginnings and names (**C**arlos, **C**at), full stops, question marks, quotation marks, commas, ellipses